PUBLISHED BY PETER HADDOCK LTD
BRIDLINGTON ENGLAND
© PETER HADDOCK LTD
Printed in Italy
ISBN 0 7105 0345 8

THE PIED PIPER
of Hamelin

Retold & Illustrated by
John Patience

Long ago, the pretty little town of Hamelin in Germany suffered from a terrible plague of vermin. The town was overrun by huge rats. They scuttled over the tiled roof tops, infested cellars and found their way into every larder in the town. They ate their way through barrels of apples, devoured cheeses by the dozen and gobbled up the grain which the towns-folk had stored up for the Winter.

The rats were bold as brass and feared no one. They stole the food from tables, fought with the dogs and cats and bit the babies in their cradles. Naturally, the people of Hamelin did everything they could to get rid of the pests. They smoked them out of their holes and put poison down for them. But it was all to no avail. Every day that passed, the rats increased in number, growing fatter as the people grew thinner. All day and all night Hamelin was filled with the deafening noise of the rats squealing and gnawing, so that there was not forty winks of sleep to be had in the whole town.

At last, the townsfolk could stand it no longer. They marched in a great crowd to the Town Hall and demanded angrily that the Mayor and his Council should do something about the vermin. But what could they do?

The Mayor and the Councillors were afraid of the angry mob and of losing their jobs. They loved their beautiful fur-lined cloaks, their gold chains and the feeling of importance which these things gave them. "Surely someone can think of a way of ridding us of the rats," cried the Mayor. "We will offer a reward to the man who can come up with the answer." The Councillors agreed that this was a good idea.

So, the very next day a town crier was sent out to read a proclamation in the town square. He rang his bell and shouted loudly:

"THERE WILL BE A REWARD OF ONE THOUSAND GILDERS FOR WHOEVER IS ABLE TO RID HAMELIN OF ITS PLAGUE OF RATS."

Well, as you know, everyone was already trying to get rid of the rats, but now they tried even harder. Rat catchers came from all over Germany to try their luck. Huge traps were dug out and baited with giant cheeses, clever chemists concocted bubbling poisons to pour down the rat holes, but still the rats infested the town!

The people of Hamelin soon began to complain again. "What use are a Mayor and Councilors in fine robes if they cannot rid us of the rats?" they wailed. Once more they marched to the Town Hall and beat upon the door. Inside the Mayor and his Council shook with fear.

Suddenly a great gust of wind blew through the hall, swirling around the marble pillars, and in the middle of it appeared a tall, thin stranger.

He was dressed in a most peculiar fashion, half in red and half in yellow. In his cap he wore a peacock feather. A mysterious smile played upon his lips, his eyes twinkled with a strange light and in his hand he carried a long, thin pipe.

"Who are you?" exclaimed the startled Mayor. "People call me the Pied Piper," answered the stranger. "I have come from halfway round the world to solve your problem and claim the reward. By means of my magic pipe I can rid Hamelin of its rats — no creature upon the earth can resist my music." The Mayor welcomed him warmly and begged him to begin his work at once, promising him not one thousand gilders but one hundred thousand if he succeeded.

The Pied Piper stepped out into the streets and began to play his music, dancing off lightly over the cobblestones. Then the rats began to appear, pouring like a squealing tide out of the houses; large rats, small rats, young rats, old rats, following the Piper as though their lives depended on it.

On and on the Piper danced all the way across the town, with the rats surging behind him, until at last he reached the River Weser. There he stepped into a boat and, continuing to play, he floated out over the deep, dark waters. After him came the rats. Pushing blindly to the river's edge, they threw themselves in. All through the night the Piper's music could be heard, accompanied by the terrible sounds of splashing and squealing, until by sunrise every last rat in Hamelin had been drowned.

That morning there was a great celebration in the town. But when the Pied Piper appeared in the Town Hall to claim his reward, no one appeared at all glad to see him. "One thousand gilders," laughed the Mayor, "that was merely a joke. Come take fifty." "One thousand gilders you promised," shouted the Pied Piper angrily, "and if you do not pay me you will soon wish you had. I can pipe other tunes as you will find out." "Go blow on your pipe until you burst," sneered the Mayor.

"Very well," said the Piper with a sinister smile. Then once again he stepped into the street and blew upon his magic pipe. This time the air was filled with a very different sort of music. It was strange and enchanting, better than the best fairy tale ever told. It was music which no child could resist. They came out from their houses laughing and chattering, not knowing where the Piper and his music would lead them, but happy and eager to follow.

The townspeople could only stand and watch, frozen like statues by the enchantment of the music. Soon every child in Hamelin was following the Piper and it looked as if he was leading them down to the River Weser. "Are we to see our children drowned?" thought the horrified parents. But no, as they watched the Piper turned west towards Koppelberg Hill. Then a great sigh of relief went up from Hamelin. "He can't possibly lead our children over Koppelberg," thought the people. "The hill is far too steep. He will surely have to stop."

But, unbelievably, as he advanced the side of the hill opened up before him and the Piper, followed by the children, disappeared inside. Then the hill closed up again, crashing together with a sound like thunder.

Only one child was left behind – a little lame boy who had not been able to keep up with the rest. He returned home sad and disappointed, knowing that he would never see the enchanted land the music had promised to lead him to.

Without the children, Hamelin was a quiet, unhappy place for many years afterwards. The Mayor and his Council were chased out of the town and a warning was carved on a stone by Koppelberg Hill that a promise once made should always be kept, especially if it is made to a piper dressed in red and yellow.